"Hey, Krissy," I called to the closed bathroom door. "Let's get a tortilla downstairs before we go shopping, okay?"

There was no response.

"Krissy, are you almost ready?" I called out.

When there was still no answer, I turned the knob and opened the door. She wasn't there. The room was empty.

I suddenly felt sick inside. Had someone kidnapped Krissy? Where could they have taken her? What should I do? Should I call my dad or the police?

I took a deep breath. I knew I wasn't thinking very well. Why would someone want to do this to Krissy? What if I never saw her again?

Look for these other books in the Forever Friends Club series:

#1 Let's Be Friends Forever!
#2 Friends to the Rescue!
#3 Keeping Secrets, Keeping Friends!
#4 That's What Friends Are For!
#5 Friends Save the Day!
#6 New Friend Blues

More Than Just A Friend

Cindy Savage

Cover illustration by Richard Kriegler

For Krissy—
who is as much a member of our family
as the character who is her namesake

Published by Willowisp Press, Inc.
401 E. Wilson Bridge Road, Worthington, Ohio 43085

Printed in the United States of America
10 9 8 7 6 5 4 3 2 1

ISBN 0-87406-447-3

One

"WOW! Just listen to that music, Aimee," Krissy said as she flopped down across her bed. "It's a real live mariachi band. It sounds so...so Mexican."

"Boy, you're quick," I said with a giggle. "Mexican music in Mexico. That seems about right to me."

"Well, I just can't believe that we're really here! I never thought I'd be in Mexico."

"I can't believe we're here either," I admitted. "Everything is so different from Atlanta. People dress so casually, and it seems like everyone moves more slowly around here. It's great."

"And just look at this place we're staying in! It's gorgeous!" Krissy said as she propped herself against the wall with a pillow.

Krissy and I were sharing a beautiful hotel room that had a huge balcony. My dad was staying in a room by himself just down the hall. My mom had decided to stay at home with my brothers. She figured that Dad would be busy working most of the time anyway.

The Hacienda Hotel had two pools, a hot tub, and a volleyball court. And we heard the restaurant had great food! We were even allowed to order room service if we felt like it.

"This is the greatest, Aimee," Krissy said. "I'm so glad that you invited me to come along with you and your dad."

"I'm so glad your parents gave their permission for you to come," I said. "Just think, we have a whole week to explore all the sights! Hey, let's go check out the view from the balcony."

I slid open the glass door and stepped outside onto the cement. Two blue chairs and a small round table sat in the corner. I walked over to the edge of the balcony and glanced down. Suddenly, I felt light-headed and my stomach did flip flops.

"Wow, we're way up here," I said. "It makes me dizzy!"

"Just be glad that we're not on the 20th

floor," Krissy pointed out. "We're only on the seventh."

I looked down again, steadying myself by holding onto the railing. The balcony overlooked the white sandy beach of Veracruz. There were colorful sailboats bobbing in the turquoise ocean. People were stretched out on beach towels everywhere. Some were relaxing at the hotel pools, and others were enjoying the sandy shore.

"Those plants are so neat," Krissy said, pointing to the palm trees and birds of paradise plants that lined the beach. "The air even smells like flowers and fruit."

"It does. I just can't wait to see more of Veracruz," I said.

"Me, neither. Now that school is finally out, all I care about is sun and sand," Krissy said.

"Yeah, it felt like school was never going to end," I groaned. "And I can't believe you got straight *A*s again. Sometimes you can be so disgusting, Kristina Branch!" Then I grinned to let her know that I was kidding.

"Thanks a lot," Krissy replied. "It's not always easy to get *A*s, you know. I was just thinking that it's too bad that Joy, Linda Jean, and Tish couldn't come to Mexico, too," Krissy said, changing the subject.

"I think I would've been asking for too much if I said I had four friends to bring along," I pointed out. "The TV studio would've lost money for sure. And, besides, you're my very best friend. So the choice was easy."

Krissy smiled. "Thanks, Aimee. That means a lot. But I can't help thinking about what we'd be doing if the others were here. I bet Joy would be out there dancing in the sand. And Linda Jean would be busy collecting all the weird rocks that she could find."

"Or looking for stray animals to bring home," I said with a grin.

Krissy laughed. "And Tish would probably be imitating all the different accents."

It seemed kind of strange to be talking about Joy, Linda Jean, and Tish and realize that they were so far away. Together, we were the Forever Friends Club, and we usually did things as a group. But this time it was different—this time it was just Krissy and me.

My dad is a reporter and host of *Weekend Mag*, a weekly TV talk show in Atlanta. He usually features stories about things that are happening in our city, so he doesn't travel too much. But for his July shows, my dad has decided to do segments on trendy vacation spots. Veracruz is the first place he's going to talk about on his show.

The main reason that Krissy and I came along with Dad is Mrs. Morris. She's the producer of my Dad's show and a pretty neat person. She's also Graham's mom. Graham and I do lots of things together, but he's not really my boyfriend. Maybe he will be someday. He is a great guy and a terrific friend!

Anyway, Mrs. Morris told Dad it was okay for Dad to bring us. And since I'm a volunteer at the station where my dad works, I'm going to help Dad set up his cue cards and coordinate the scripts and stuff like that. It's fun!

Besides my job at the TV studio, I also have a business with Krissy, Joy Marshall, Linda Jean Jacobs, and Tish Baker. It's called Party Time, and we entertain at kids' parties. Each of us has a special talent, so it's easy to work together as a team.

My talent is making crafts, so I come up with ideas for projects that are easy for kids to make. Krissy wears a clown suit and does magic tricks. When she puts on her silly costume, she turns into a real ham. The kids at our parties usually cheer loudest for her.

"Well, let's get going. The Forever Friends are ready to conquer Mexico!" I announced to the ocean below.

"Well, two of the Forever Friends anyway," Krissy added. "But we'll make up for the others!"

I walked back into the room and began taking my clothes out of my suitcase and hanging them up in the huge closet.

"We'll just have to do everything we've planned to do and take lots of pictures," I said to Krissy. "Then when we show the pictures to the rest of the Forever Friends they will feel like they were here with us!"

I waved the long list of places we'd planned to go and things we'd planned to see that we had written up together during the flight to Mexico. We had brought along three sightseeing books, an entertainment guide, and a Spanish/English dictionary just in case we needed it.

"Okay, but I want to get some sun first," Krissy said, looking down at her arms. "I'm so pale."

"Sure, but we can't lie in the sun all day. There are so many places to go and people to see and art exhibits to explore."

"I know. But I do want to get a tan while I'm here," Krissy said.

"You'll get your tan. Don't worry," I assured her. "And maybe after the big party in the ballroom tonight, we'll even know how to do a party south-of-the-border style."

"Yeah, that would be a nice change from all the dinosaur and monster parties we've put on," Krissy said, looking deep in thought.

"Is something wrong?" I asked her when she didn't say anything for a while.

"No, I was just thinking. Sometimes I wonder what it'd be like *not* to be a part of the Forever Friends. I mean, I really don't know what I'd do without you guys."

I hung up my new pair of jeans and turned around to look at her. "Well, that's not something you have to worry about, is it?" I asked. I knew I was looking at Krissy strangely, but I had no idea why she was talking like that.

"It's just that things are changing. Next year I'll be going to the high school, and I won't be with you every day anymore." Krissy was a grade ahead of the rest of us in the club. She had skipped a grade when she was little because she was so smart.

"Yeah, but we'll still have our meetings

every day after school," I added quickly. "That's not going to change."

"But what about boys?" Krissy asked. "All of you already have boys you like. You always talk about the fun you have with Graham at the TV station. And Linda Jean sees Nick once in a while at the skating rink. Even Joy is all excited because Russell wrote to her about his performance this summer at the Fox Theater downtown."

Finally, I realized what Krissy was really talking about. We were the ones with boys, and she felt like she didn't belong anymore. She felt like we were all moving in different directions.

"Krissy, you'll have a boyfriend before you know it," I said. "And it's really no big deal with Graham and me. He's great, but it's not like we see each other all the time. Besides, pretty soon, you'll have guys flocking all around you. What guy can resist a cute blond?"

She giggled. "Oh, stop it, Aimee. Most of the eighth graders think I'm a baby because I skipped a grade and am younger than they are. And if they don't see me as a baby, they think I'm the nerdy brain type."

"It can't be that bad," I insisted.

Krissy shrugged her shoulders. "Well, it's not like that all the time. But I wish I could be beautiful and have a great boy to like me. Sounds like a dream, doesn't it?"

"No, it'll happen. Just wait and see," I said. "Hey, we're going to a fancy ball tonight. Maybe Prince Charming will be lurking somewhere in the shadows."

We both giggled as we started getting ready for the big ball. This was going to be a great trip and a great night. I just knew it!

Two

THE ball was being held in the open-air courtyard of the hotel where we were staying. The hotel had recently been renovated by Jasper Stark, the man who owned the hotel. He was also our host during our visit.

Krissy and I took one last peek at ourselves in the mirror before we headed down to the ball. The hotel manager had sent up authentic Mexican dresses for us to wear. The dresses were so colorful and full and they made us feel elegant and graceful.

"Wow! You look beautiful, Krissy," I said.

"Thanks. This dress makes me feel special," she said. "You look great, too!"

We met my dad at his room and went downstairs together. Mr. Stark greeted us at the arched entry that led into the garden.

"*Bienvenido*, welcome my friends," Mr. Stark said. "I hope you are rested from your trip, because we're going to keep you entertained far into the night."

"That sounds great," Dad said to Mr. Stark. "I'd like you to meet my daughter, Aimee. And this is her friend, Kristina Branch. I'm sure these girls will be paying close attention to your party tonight, because they have their own party business back home. They just may pick up a few good ideas here from you."

"I am charmed," Mr. Stark told us. "I would love to hear what you think of our party. I am always open to new ideas and suggestions. I especially like to hear what young people have to say. I want to make this hotel a special place for our guests, so they'll remember it when they come back to Veracruz again."

We smiled politely. "Sure, Mr. Stark, we'd be glad to tell you what we think," I offered.

"Thanks, girls. My teenage son, Jim, helps me out sometimes with the business," Mr. Stark explained. "But I know that he'd rather be hanging around the beach or out sailing."

I smiled. "Well, let us know what we can do to help you out," I said as I glanced around the room.

I watched as people in traditional Mexican clothing wandered around the room looking for a place to sit. We passed by the buffet table, and I could smell all kinds of Mexican foods.

"Everything sure smells great," I whispered to Krissy. She nodded and pointed to the band that was setting up to play.

"Maybe we'll be able to find some guys to dance with us tonight," she whispered with a giggle.

"I had planned to introduce you to Jim," Mr. Stark said. "But I don't see him anywhere right now. When I find him, I'll bring him over to meet you."

"Sure, that would be nice," Dad said with a grin in our direction. He knew that we would never turn down the chance to meet a teen-age boy. "Jasper, you definitely picked a great spot to buy a hotel. It's so peaceful around here."

"Yes, we love our time here. But we spend six months of the year in the U.S., too. I have a hotel business in Maine that I have to keep track of."

I tuned out of their conversation. I had promised Dad that I'd help him with cue cards and stuff like that, but interviewing Mr. Stark wasn't part of my job.

Dad had asked Krissy and me to mingle with some of the other kids who were on vacation. He wanted us to find out what they thought about Veracruz and the Hacienda Hotel. I looked around at the kids who were eating dinner and decided not to bother anyone tonight. There would be plenty of time tomorrow to talk to kids at the pool or on the beach.

Krissy and I excused ourselves from Dad and Mr. Stark. We walked around the room to check out all of the cool decorations. Every corner was different. Giant red, gold, and purple paper flowers filled a huge basket vase in one corner. In another, bright ponchos and straw hats were draped over cane chairs.

Most of the guests were wearing authentic Mexican outfits. The women wore long, colorful dresses. The men wore black charro outfits with ruffled shirts, silver embroidery, and shiny black boots.

We got in line for the buffet, piled food on our plates, and found a table where we could sit down to eat.

"Oh, look," Krissy said, pointing toward the stage. "The dancers are getting ready."

"Hey, some of them look like they're our age!" I exclaimed. "We should take a picture of them for Joy. She'd love it! And I bet next she'll be wanting to do that local dance I read about. It's called *Baile Folklorico*."

The dancers dipped and swayed as they danced. Their heels clicked every time they moved around the floor. The music was really fast and even wild in parts. I had no idea how the dancers kept up with the beat of the music. I knew I'd look like a human pretzel if I tried to dance like that!

I was busy eating my dinner when I looked up at Krissy. She seemed hypnotized or something. Then I noticed that it wasn't the dance she was staring at. There was one special dancer who had captured her attention.

"He's cute, isn't he?" I asked her.

"Watch how fast his feet move," she whispered to me. "He looks so happy. Hey, look. He's smiling at us."

"He's smiling at everyone," I said. "He's a performer. It's his job to make you feel like he's performing only for you."

Why would she think he was smiling only at us? I wondered. The idea seemed a little crazy to me.

"This is different," Krissy insisted. "I think he likes me."

The dance was over and a new one started up. The same boy stayed on stage and began to dance again. He performed the Mexican Hat Dance, which the Mexicans call the *Jarabe Tapatio*, and a dance called *Chiampanecas.*

I watched the boy's eyes and saw that he did glance over at Krissy a lot. And when she smiled at him, he smiled back. *Maybe Krissy wasn't imagining things after all.*

"Let's go meet him," I suggested when the dancers finally took a break.

Krissy yanked at my arm before I had taken two steps. "Are you kidding? I'm not going up there and make a fool of myself. No way! I'm sure you were right, Aimee. I was just imagining that he was smiling at me."

She spun around and headed quickly toward the dessert table. I shrugged my shoulders and followed her across the room. I had to convince Krissy that she should try to be bolder about this. If she liked the dancer, then maybe she should go and meet him.

We each picked up a hand-painted pottery plate and loaded up on goodies—pan dulce, flan, bunuelos, chispas. Each dish had a sign above it that described the ingredients.

"You should try the torte," a voice said smoothly behind us. "It melts in your mouth. Really."

We both turned to find the cute dancer smiling at us. Krissy just stared at him, so I figured I'd better say something.

"Hi. You were great up there," I said.

Krissy almost dropped her flan. "Hello," she said finally.

"I'm glad you enjoyed it," he said. "I love performing with the dance troupe whenever I'm in Mexico. I miss it when I go back to the States."

"You live in the United States?" Krissy asked.

The boy flashed Krissy a 1000 watt smile. "Yes, in Maine." Then he added, "Oh, I'm sorry. I haven't introduced myself. I'm Jim Stark."

Jim had beautiful brown hair and a terrific tan. His eyes sparkled when he talked, and his teeth seemed to be perfectly white.

"Oh, you're Mr. Stark's son. He mentioned you earlier, but he didn't say that you were a dancer," I said.

"Surprise!" Jim said dramatically.

Krissy giggled.

Oh, brother, I thought. *Was Krissy really going to fall for this guy's charm act? I knew I should be nice to him, since my dad was focusing his story around this hotel. But for some reason, Jim seemed a little too charming to me.*

Krissy didn't seem to notice. For the rest of the evening Jim stayed with us. He decided to be our personal host. He took us on a grand tour of the Hacienda, including the suite of rooms where his family lived. He told us all about the fancy hotels his father owned along the coast of Maine. I guess we were supposed to be impressed.

"Do you know what Veracruz means?" he asked, handing each of us a crystal cup filled with punch from the buffet table.

We shook our heads. But I knew we were about to hear the whole story.

"When Hernan Cortes landed here on Good Friday in 1519, he named the town Villa Rica de la Vera Cruz. That means rich town of the True Cross," Jim said.

"That's beautiful," Krissy said sweetly. "So, why did they shorten it?"

"I guess because it's too much of a mouthful to say all of that," Jim said with a laugh.

"You speak Spanish very well," Krissy added. "Especially when you roll your *R*s."

Jim ran a hand through his perfectly combed hair. He brushed his bangs off of his forehead. "Well, my father is American, and my mother is part Mexican. I've lived in each country at some point in my life."

"Wow. That must be neat," Krissy said. "I've never been farther than South Carolina."

"Yes, you have. You're in Mexico now, aren't you?" Jim asked smoothly. "Hey, let's have some fun." With that, he grabbed Krissy's hand and led her onto the dance floor. The mariachi band was belting out a fast song. I watched as Krissy giggled and blushed her way around the floor as she tried to follow his fancy steps.

Just as I was feeling disgusted by the whole thing, Jim danced Krissy over toward me. Then he took my hand and soon we were all dancing and laughing together.

After two songs, he introduced us to some of the other kids who were staying at the hotel. We spent the next hour talking about where everyone came from and what they liked to do. Dad sure was going to be thrilled. I'd learned a lot of different things that he could talk about on his TV show.

When the band finally took a break, Jim stood up. "Wait right here," he said. "I just have to go talk to my father for a minute."

"We'll be here," Krissy promised. Her eyes followed him as he made his way over toward his dad. "Isn't he wonderful?" she whispered.

"Krissy, he must be at least 15 or 16," I pointed out.

"So? Aren't his eyes gorgeous?" she asked. "And he's a great dancer. I'm having so much fun!"

I grinned. I thought Krissy was being silly about this guy. I mean, she'd only met him an hour ago! But it was great to see her so happy, especially after she had sounded so worried about the Forever Friends growing apart. "I have to go find the ladies' room," I said. "Will you be okay for a couple of minutes?"

"Of course, Aimee," Krissy replied. "Stop looking so serious. I'm going to get a different dessert. I didn't like the pudding. Besides, I'll need energy when the band starts up again."

Right, I thought sarcastically. I admit that I had fun dancing with Jim and Krissy. And Jim seemed to be nice enough. Maybe I was worried about Krissy liking him too much. I didn't want to see her get hurt when we had to go back to Atlanta.

Before I left the restroom, I combed my hair and readjusted my Mexican dress. I couldn't figure out why Jim got on my nerves, but he did. All I could hope for was that he'd leave Krissy alone after the dance. I didn't want the three of us hanging out together for the whole week. I opened the door and headed down the hallway.

As I walked toward our table, I noticed that Jim was sitting next to Krissy again. She looked absolutely dazzled as Jim led her out onto the dance floor for a fast dance.

I wanted Krissy to be happy. But seeing her with this guy really bothered me. I couldn't understand it. And there was no easy way to tell your best friend that you think her first major crush is a creep.

Three

I woke up early the next morning. The sunshine was streaming through the window, and I'd forgotten to shut the drapes the night before. I guess I had been too busy worrying about Krissy and Jim to think about anything else.

I walked out onto the balcony and looked down. A few people were already getting comfortable by the pool. It was nice to relax on vacation, but lying in the sun seemed so boring to me. We had come all the way to Mexico, and there was so much to see and do! Convincing Krissy of that, though, sure wasn't going to be easy.

I sat down on one of the chairs and propped my feet up on the balcony railing. I was tired from tossing in my sleep all night. I couldn't stop thinking about Krissy and Jim.

I had spent most of the evening sitting at our table. I had watched the two of them dance and giggle for an hour before I decided to head up to our room.

Maybe today would be better. Maybe Jim would be busy working with his father and then Krissy and I could have some fun exploring the city together.

"Good morning," Krissy said cheerfully as she joined me on the balcony. "Isn't this absolutely the best vacation?"

"Mexico is definitely neat all right," I agreed quickly. "And I would love to see lots more of it while I'm here."

"I get your point," Krissy said. "Don't worry, Aimee. I promise not to be a tanning freak the whole time. Okay? Just let me get some sun this morning, and then we can do some exploring this afternoon."

I sighed. "Okay. That sounds fair enough."

We called room service and ordered breakfast. I was starved from all the dancing we had done with Jim and the other kids the night before.

In less than 10 minutes, the waiter arrived and wheeled the table as close to the balcony as he could. We had freshly baked sweet bread and fresh-squeezed grapefruit juice. We sat quietly and listened to the ocean while we ate.

"Okay, I'll be ready to go in a couple of minutes," I said as I headed into the room to find my new swimsuit and beach bag.

"Me, too," Krissy said. She pulled her shorts on over her swimsuit and stepped into her sandals. "I'm so glad we decided to spend our first morning here at the beach."

"Yeah, I can read some of the book I bought at the airport," I said. "Then we'll be ready to shop at the market later. Dad should be busy all day setting up background shots and appointments, so I don't think I'll have any work to do."

"So, which sights are you really excited about seeing, Aimee?" Krissy asked as we headed down to the beach.

"Well, I really want to go into town to see that museum on Zaragoza Street," I said. "The guidebook said that it used to be an orphanage. It sounds pretty neat. And Mr. Stark said that the museum has rooms filled with regional costumes and crafts. I'd love to find out about the crafts."

"I'm sure kids at home would love to learn

how to make Mexican crafts," Krissy said. "Hey, I wonder what I could do to make my act Mexican, too. Do you think they have clowns in Mexico?"

"I guess we could ask somebody," I suggested.

"Maybe Jim would know," Krissy said with a smile. "And if we're really going to do a party with a Mexican theme, we should find out all we can now so that it will be really authentic."

"Yeah, *if* we see Jim," I muttered under my breath.

I was really hoping that I'd seen the last of Jim Stark, but I knew we'd see him again. After all, it was his job to be nice to all the hotel guests. Maybe that was the problem. I sort of felt like he was being extra sweet to us so that Dad would give the Hacienda Hotel a lot of news coverage on his TV show. Well, Jim wasn't a good enough actor for me.

Then, suddenly, I was mad at myself. Who was I to judge Jim? Maybe I *was* jealous. Maybe I missed having Graham around to pay attention to me. He always knew how to cheer me up and make me feel special just when I needed it. He was really great about that kind of thing.

We walked down the tile walkway and

slipped off our shoes as soon as we reached the sand. People were quickly filling up every spare inch of the beach in front of the hotel. We headed out toward some rocks that jutted out into the ocean.

We found a tiny path that led through the rocks and trees. We made our way along the path and ended up finding a narrow stretch of beach. We both jumped down from the last rock and looked around. We had found a gorgeous deserted cove. It was like having our own private beach!

"This beach was made just for us!" Krissy shouted. She quickly dropped her beach bag and towel and pulled off her shorts and T-shirt. She dove right into the water. The waves were so calm in the cove that it felt like we had our very own Mexican swimming pool.

In less than a minute, I was splashing and paddling in the water beside Krissy. I loved floating on salt water. It made me feel like I didn't weigh anything!

"Home sure seems far away," I said. "It's so peaceful and perfect here. Atlanta could never be like this. People are always on their way somewhere at home."

Krissy nodded. "I know. I really like the

siestas that everyone takes in the afternoons here. It's amazing that all of Veracruz closes down in the afternoon for naps. Wouldn't it be great if they did that at school?"

We giggled as we pictured what that would be like.

"Hey, why don't we write a letter to the others?" I suggested. "We could write one long letter from both of us. I could write the beginning, and you can add what you want, too."

Krissy dove underwater just then and brought up an interesting shell. "Sorry, but I couldn't resist grabbing this for a souvenir," she said. "Yeah, let's write them all a letter. But we'll only have time to write one while we're here. Otherwise, we'd be back in Atlanta before the letters got there!"

We swam back to shore and spread out on the beach towels that the hotel had given us to use. I reached for my notebook and looked over at Krissy. She was busy putting on suntan lotion.

"Hey, wait a minute. I have a neat idea," Krissy said excitedly. "How about if we take turns keeping a travel diary?"

"What do you mean?" I asked her.

"Well, since we won't have a chance to write

more than one letter, we could jot things down in a diary just like we're really going to mail the letters. But instead we'll hand it to them when we get home. Then we won't forget to tell them anything important."

"That's a neat idea," I admitted. "When do you want to start on it?"

"In a little while. I'd like to relax right now," Krissy said.

I noticed that she was staring thoughtfully out at the ocean. I shoved my paper back in my beach bag and grabbed my book.

I had only read three pages when I heard boys' voices close by. I looked up from my book and saw a bunch of guys standing on our private beach.

The boys all wore long colorful shorts and T-shirts. One of them tossed a soccer ball onto the sand and kicked it to another boy.

I peered over the top of my sunglasses and watched as they expertly passed the soccer ball back and forth. I did my best to ignore them.

"Why couldn't they play soccer on another beach?" I complained to Krissy. "I mean, there are all kinds of beaches around here. Why did they have to pick ours?"

I expected her to agree, but she didn't say anything. I did a double take when I saw the look in her eyes. She seemed completely fascinated by these guys. She was watching their every move!

"Aimee, didn't your dad ask us to mingle a little?" Krissy asked. "Why don't we start with these guys? I think they're kind of cute."

I sighed. There was no use in discussing boys with Krissy. She was becoming more hopeless all the time.

Krissy giggled. "Relax and quit complaining," she said. "It's like having your very own cute guy contest right in front of you. You have to admit that these guys are good looking, Aimee. So, enjoy it!"

Enjoy it? I asked myself. *Where did this new, bold Krissy come from all of a sudden?* She was the one who had been upset about not having a boyfriend, and now she was acting like she knew all about guys!

I had told my dad that we'd be glad to mingle with some of the other kids, but I wasn't so sure this was what he meant. I shoved my sunglasses back up my nose and buried my face in my book.

Suddenly, Krissy grabbed my arm. "Hey,

don't look now," she said, "but I think one of those guys is Jim."

Oh, great! I thought. I had been looking forward to a fun day with Krissy, and now Jim was here. So much for my plans. I glanced over at the boys to see if she was right.

"Don't look!" Krissy ordered.

"How can I tell if it's Jim if I don't look?" I asked.

"Well, look, but don't look. You know what I mean. Just don't let him catch you staring at him or anything," Krissy whispered.

Boy, she was really into this Jim thing, I realized. I casually looked over to where the boys were still kicking the ball around. One of them definitely looked like Jim. *Rats!*

I knew I was being pretty selfish about the whole thing. After all, when we were home, I did see Graham pretty often. And here I was being ridiculous about Krissy having a crush on Jim. Maybe I should be more like a best friend and try to help her.

"Why don't we go swimming again?" I whispered back. "Then we can walk past the boys and into the water. We'll be able to get a closer look without being really obvious."

"Great idea," Krissy replied with a big grin.

She looked so excited that I felt badly for feeling angry about Jim. We stood up and started walking across the sand. We were almost to the water when one of the boys called out to us.

"¡Hola, muchachas! ¿Como estan?" he asked us.

Krissy leaned toward me a little. "What did he say? she asked softly.

"He asked how we are," I explained. "Hey, seventh-grade Spanish is coming in handy after all. You're supposed to answer *bien.* It means good."

Krissy turned around just as we reached the water. *"Bien,"* she said cheerfully to the group.

The boys walked closer to us and began chattering away. And there in the middle was Jim.

"Krissy, Aimee. These guys are Edwardo, Felipe, Max, Paulo, Jorqe, Rodolfo, and Pedro. They all work for my dad at the hotel."

"It's nice to meet you," I said quickly. "I'm just going in for a swim to cool off a little."

Then I dove into the water. I swam around for a few minutes and then stood up again. I saw that all of the boys except Jim had followed me into the ocean.

Krissy had stayed behind. I could hear her voice above the waves. "I really had a good time last night, Jim," she said. "Thanks for giving us the tour."

"Nothing is too good for a princess," he replied.

I saw Krissy's cheeks turn red, but she kept on talking. Her blond hair blew in the breeze. She looked really pretty and happy.

"*¿Habla español?*" one of the boys asked me. I think he was Eduardo.

"*Sí, un poco,*" I told him, meaning a little bit.

"*Me gusta hablar con las Americanas,*" he said. "*Quiero ir a la Universidad en Nueva York.*"

"Whoa! Hold on," I said as I stood there in the water trying to translate what he was saying. Did he say he wanted to attend the New York University or that he wanted to explore the universe? No, it had to be the first one!

We talked back and forth the rest of the morning. Jim helped to translate the words that I didn't understand. We learned that most of the boys were in high school. They worked for Mr. Stark after school and on weekends.

I watched as Krissy talked and laughed and seemed to have a great time. She usually stayed away from older boys because she said they made her nervous. This sure was a new Krissy Branch!

I thought back to what Krissy had said in our hotel room the first night. She was right. Things were changing—and fast.

By lunchtime, I was exhausted. I hadn't slept well the night before, and I'd just spent three hours trying to talk in Spanish. I found out that learning how to say whole conversations during Spanish class didn't help at all in the real world!

I noticed that Krissy was whispering to Jim. I knew she was having fun, but I couldn't help feeling like she was ignoring me. We had planned to spend the whole day together. And now here sat the 10 of us.

"We'd better head back," I said to Krissy. "We can change our clothes and get some lunch before we go to the market."

"Uh, Aimee," Krissy said hesitantly. "Jim invited us to go out on his sailboat. Isn't that great?" When I didn't say anything, she asked, "You want to go, don't you?"

Jim gave me one of his perfect smiles.

"That's my boat right out there in the harbor. See the bright blue and white sail. It's new and really safe," he assured me.

"I think I'll pass," I said. I did not return his smile. "I'm going to go to the market this afternoon—like we had planned. You guys go ahead though."

Krissy looked from me to Jim and back again. "No, I don't want to go without you," she said.

"I don't mind, really," I told her. But I did mind. I felt really disappointed. I had wanted to spend time with her on this trip or I wouldn't have invited her to come. But I would just have to live with it. "I'll see everybody later," I said as I started to walk away.

Suddenly, I heard footsteps and then Krissy was walking beside me.

"Dummy," she said, punching my arm affectionately. "Of course I'm going with you to the market. That was the plan."

I grinned, letting my relief show on my face. "We're going to have a great time while we're here," I said.

Krissy looked back at the guys and waved. "I'm having a great time already!"

Four

"I'M beat," I said as I flopped across my bed half an hour later. "And I'm starved. But it feels good just to lie here for a few minutes."

Krissy was staring out of the balcony window. I figured she was trying to spot Jim's boat sailing somewhere in the ocean.

"Hey, I think I see it!" she said excitedly. She pointed out toward the water.

"You see what?" I asked, pretending not to know what she was talking about.

"Jim's boat. Boy, sailing sure looks like fun!" she said with a grin.

I didn't say anything. I just closed my eyes. "Hey, why don't we rest for a little while? Then we can head down to the market and buy out the place," I suggested.

"That sounds good," Krissy agreed as she

sat down on her bed. "Maybe we'll get to go sailing later this week."

"Maybe," I said. "There are lots of other things to do, too. Remember that we're going to the ruins at Zempoala and Tajin tomorrow. I can't wait to see them. They're supposed to be really cool ancient stone temples."

"Sure," Krissy said. "Hey, you speak those Spanish words pretty well. I wish I'd taken Spanish instead of French last year."

"Spanish is really easy," I said. "I'll teach you some while we're at the market this afternoon, okay? I can point out things and give you the Spanish word for them, too. I don't think I could carry on long conversations with anybody, especially since they speak so fast. But I can pick out words that I learned in class."

"Do you think the Mexicans are insulted if you say things wrong?" Krissy asked.

"They're probably glad that you try to speak their language," I said. "It's nicer than just expecting them to speak to you in English. Hey, maybe I'll learn so much that I can skip a semester of Spanish."

Krissy giggled. "I don't think Mr. Dymski would go for that, do you?"

"Probably not," I admitted.

"Jim speaks English and Spanish perfectly. It's amazing that he can switch back and forth between living in Mexico and Maine like that," Krissy said. "You'd think it would be really hard to do."

"I guess it's easy to do if it's something that you're used to," I said, hoping that she wasn't going to start daydreaming about Jim again.

Part of me felt like I had ruined Krissy's chance of a lifetime. She had met a guy who she really liked, and he had invited her to spend the day sailing. I did have to admit that it sounded like a lot of fun. But something inside made me feel sick when I thought about the two of them sailing off without me. And there was no way that I would have gone with them. I definitely would have been in the way.

"Yeah, Jim's life must be exciting," Krissy said with a big grin. "Can you imagine having a father who owns all those hotels? You'd get to travel everywhere and meet all kinds of neat people. Wow!"

"Yeah, but you'd always be behind in school. That's something I can't imagine you doing, Krissy," I said.

"Well, I think could handle it for a little

while," Krissy added with a smile.

"Since our dads don't have jobs like Jim's does, let's make the most of Mexico while we are here, okay?" I tried again. "Maybe after the market we could go to the promenade."

"What's that again?" Krissy asked.

"It's where people go to enjoy the sunset or the moonlight. I hear it's really romantic," I said, realizing I might have said the wrong thing.

"Hmm. I bet sailing is, too," Krissy said.

We stopped talking and my mind kept spinning with visions of all the sights I wanted to see. Soon, my eyelids grew heavy and I couldn't stay awake.

I awoke to the smell of freshly made tortillas. I stretched and sat up on my bed. I looked over at Krissy's bed, but she wasn't there. I figured she was getting ready to go shopping. I looked at my watch and saw that I'd been asleep for an hour.

I walked out onto the balcony and watched the women working in the courtyard below. I could see that their hands were moving rapidly as they patted and pressed the tortillas into place on the metal presses. I realized that I was really hungry now.

"Hey, Krissy," I called to the closed bathroom door. "Let's get a tortilla downstairs before we head out, okay?"

I walked over to the mirror and began brushing my hair. Then I picked out my most colorful T-shirt and shorts to wear. I hoped Krissy would hurry up or we'd never see anything.

"Krissy, are you almost done in there?" I called out.

There was no response.

I walked over to the bathroom door and knocked. When there was still no answer, I turned the knob and opened the door. She wasn't there. The room was empty!

I suddenly felt sick inside. Had someone kidnapped Krissy? Where could they have taken her? What should I do? Should I call my dad, the police, or Mr. Stark? I couldn't believe this was happening! Why would someone want to do this to Krissy? What if I never saw her again?

I knew I wasn't thinking very well. Maybe Krissy had gone for a walk. Maybe she couldn't sleep and decided to look around while I took a nap. *Yeah, maybe that was it,* I decided. But I couldn't be sure of that.

I ran back out onto the balcony and quickly scanned the courtyard below. I figured her blond hair would be easy to spot even from the seventh floor. I saw other kids roaming around, but none of them looked like Krissy.

I looked on and under her pillow. Krissy or the kidnappers could have left a note. But there was nothing there.

I scribbled a note to Krissy, asking her to wait in the room if she did come back.

I ran to the closest elevator and pressed the button for the lobby. As the elevator slowly descended, I could hear my heartbeat thumping in my ears.

I searched through the shops in the hotel, then headed out into the streets. I couldn't find Krissy anywhere. I knew that I had to tell someone what had happened.

I ran to the hotel phone and called my dad's room. I let it ring eight times before I hung up. *He must be doing more interviews,* I thought. I walked back into the courtyard and asked everyone I passed if they had noticed a pretty blond girl.

"*¿Ha visto, Usted, una chica rubia? Es mi amiga, Kristina. No puedo encontrarla,*" I told everyone. It means, "Have you seen a blond girl? She's my friend, Kristina, and I can't find her."

After 10 minutes of shaking heads and sad looks from the people, I felt even more frightened.

"This is ridiculous," I told myself. "She has to be around here somewhere."

I took the elevator back up to our floor and walked down the hallway. If she wasn't in our room, I was going to call security. They could check out the hotel a lot faster than I could.

I took a deep breath, hoping that Krissy would be sitting on her bed. I slowly opened the door. Everything was just as I had left it. My note was still on her pillow. I was scared.

I couldn't stop the tears from running down my cheeks. I ran over to the phone on the table near the balcony doors. I picked up the receiver and dialed for the hotel operator.

"*Sí?*" the operator asked, meaning "yes."

I couldn't think of what to say in Spanish. My tongue felt like it was tangled in my mouth. I finally told her in English what had happened. She said she'd have security call me right back.

I stepped onto the balcony to scan the courtyard one more time. Then I saw it! It was

Jim's bright blue-and-white sail just off shore. And the bright rainbow colors on deck were unmistakable. It was Krissy's swimsuit. I could see her blond hair blowing in the wind. And she looked like she was laughing.

Suddenly, all my fears vanished. And I was furious! I was angry and hurt that she would do this to me. I had spent almost an hour looking around for her. I had called hotel security because I thought that she might be in trouble. And here she had snuck off to see Jim while I was sleeping!

"Thanks a lot, Krissy," I said to myself. I grabbed the note off of her pillow and crunched it into a little ball.

Some best friend she's turning out to be! I thought as I slammed out of our hotel room.

Five

I bought a fresh tortilla from the women in the hotel courtyard for lunch. Then I jumped on the first bus into town. I picked a seat near the back so I didn't have to talk to anyone. I definitely needed some time to cool down over my anger with Krissy.

The 15-minute ride to the market took us through some neat places. We passed people selling crafts and jewelry along the street. I saw that some of the homes in Veracruz were really nice and others were really run-down. The further the bus rode away from Krissy and Jim, the better I felt.

I looked at the woman who was sitting in front of me and saw that she was carrying a whole bagful of brightly-colored mats. I had to concentrate to come up with the right

Spanish words to speak with her.

"How do you make those?" I finally asked her in Spanish.

The woman saw that I was an American and did her best to answer me in English. For the rest of our ride into town, she explained how she spun wool from her own sheep and wove the wool by using a small tapestry loom. From her description, it sounded like the loom was something like a picture frame with nails on it.

"¿Cuanto cuesta?" I asked to find out the price of her mats.

The woman told me her price in pesos, and I quickly calculated it into American dollars. I couldn't believe how cheap they were! She was selling each mat for $2.50.

"Quiero dos," I said, telling her that I wanted two mats. I took some pesos out of my purse and handed them to her. "Muchas gracias," I said to thank her.

Soon, I saw the market in front of us. I was excited to go exploring. I felt a lot better than I had 15 minutes earlier. Krissy could have Mr. Jim the Charmer if she wanted him. I would have fun and go exploring without her.

I hopped off the bus and admired the big

sign over the door to the market. In bold letters, it said, *"Mercado Central,"* meaning Central Market.

The guidebook had said that the market was a big bargaining center. That meant that all the items didn't have prices on them. You didn't pick out something and then pay for it, like you did back home. Instead, you asked for their price and then offered to pay the person what you thought the item was worth. You bargained with them until you both agreed on a price.

But as I walked up and down the aisles, it didn't seem fair to cheat these people out of money. I guess it wasn't cheating exactly, but I was used to paying a lot more at home for things that weren't as neat as this stuff was.

The craftsmanship was wonderful. I could tell that some of the crafts had taken hours to make. And the merchants were only asking a few pennies for their work.

I looked up and realized that I blended into the crowd easily with my dark hair and dark eyes. It felt great just to wander around and become absorbed in this new culture. I tried to pretend that I really lived here, that I was a Veracruzana and not an American.

"*Señorita,*" a woman called out to me. "I have fresh oranges right from the tree. Very sweet. Come take a taste."

I walked closer to the pretty woman and took a section of an orange. She was right. The oranges were the best I'd ever had! I bought three.

I noticed that a lot of other shoppers were carrying nets to hold the stuff they had bought. I looked around until I found a stand that sold them. I decided to buy two nets. I thought my mom might like to have one as a souvenir.

I wandered up one aisle and down the other. One man and a boy who looked like he must be the man's son were selling handwoven rugs and blankets. Another man sold dried peppers in long strings and bunches of dried herbs. He told me that the yellow flowers were called manzanilla and were used to make chamomile tea.

All kinds of sounds and smells meshed together around me. I was having a great time—until I saw a boy running down the next aisle carrying a live chicken by its feet!

"Do you like animals?" a young girl asked from the table next to me. I guess she wanted to make sure I was all right. I was definitely not used to seeing live chickens being carried around on the street like that! It seemed pretty weird to me.

"Oh, you speak English," I said gratefully.

"Yes, some," the girl replied. "I like to learn as much as I can."

"Me, too," I said. "I know a little Spanish from school. My name is Aimee."

"I am Ciela," she said.

"Do you live near here?" I asked her.

"Yes, on Lerdo Street near the Plaza de Armas. And you?"

"I'm from Atlanta, Georgia," I explained. "I'm here because my father is going to talk about Veracruz on a TV show that he does. I have some friends at home who would love your crafts. Maybe I could take some back to them. Which are your favorites?"

We had a great time looking through all her animal figures. They were all made from corn husks. I picked out a bird for Linda Jean and a kitten for Joy. And I found a little mouse for Tish in honor of her cartoon character imitations.

"I work, too," I told her after we'd been talking for a while.

"My friends and I give parties for children," I explained. Talking about Party Time made me think about the Forever Friends Club. And thinking about the Forever Friends made me think about how mad I was at Krissy. But I decided to put Krissy out of my mind for now. I was having fun talking to Ciela.

"My job is to show kids how to make crafts," I continued. "Do you think kids could make animals like yours?"

"The corn husk animals are easy to make," she said with a smile. "Let me show you how."

I sat down on a stool beside Ciela. I watched her as she bent and wrapped wet corn husks into animal shapes. It was fascinating to watch her work. She could make an animal in about 10 minutes.

Boy, Krissy was missing out on a lot of culture, I thought angrily.

Ciela showed me how to get started on one and then spent some time helping out other customers. When she had a break, she told me all about her family.

"I have six brothers and two sisters," she said. "My father drives a truck, and my mother sells her crafts. We all try to do something to help out our family."

"It kind of sounds like my house," I told her with a grin. "I have four brothers, but that's enough!"

Ciela laughed. "Yes, brothers can be difficult."

"Yes, they can be lots of trouble," I said. "But they can be fun sometimes."

Ciela nodded. I decided that she would be a great pen pal.

"What do you think of all the new hotels along the beach?" I asked her. "Does it bother you at all?"

Ciela thought for a minute. Then she shook her head. "It's good, I guess," she said hesitantly. "Tourists bring in business and help our country. The hotels are so big and beautiful, too. My brothers work there."

"It sounds like you're not quite sure whether all of the changes will be good ones," I said. "Is that right?"

Ciela paused for a second. "Well, I think prices will go up for all of us. We will make more money, but I think it will all be the same in the end. Except we'll have more people here."

"I like the way Veracruz is now," I said to Ciela. I looked around at the rows of all the vendors selling their wares and the fun atmosphere of the market.

Ciela smiled. "I am glad to have made a new American friend," she said.

I smiled back. "Thanks for showing me how to make the animals," I said. I picked out a couple more to take home for my mom and for Joy's mom, Abby.

I handed Ciela the money for everything I'd picked out that afternoon. But she wouldn't let me pay very much.

"No," she said with a giggle. "You say you will pay half of what someone is asking. Then the seller complains about it, but slowly comes down in price. You slowly come up until you pay a price somewhere in the middle."

"That seems so weird to me," I said. "Our stores at home are not like that at all. This is almost like a game."

"Maybe, but it is important that you do it that way here," Ciela explained. "People have pride and do not want to take charity."

"I've learned a lot from you, Ciela," I said. "I would really like to hear from you sometime. Would you write to me in Georgia? I could practice my Spanish and you could practice your English."

Her eyes lit up. "Yes. That would be nice."

We exchanged addresses, and I told her that she was welcome to come and visit me anytime.

I walked over to the woman at the table across the aisle and asked if she would take our picture. I showed her how to hold my camera and shoot the picture. Ciela and I stood close together and smiled at each other. I left with a wave and a promise to write soon.

Wow, what a great day, I thought. Then I remembered seeing Krissy as she sailed along with Jim. My stomach did a flip flop as I thought about it.

I wandered down the aisles a little while longer and bought a few more souvenirs for everyone. This time I tried the bartering tricks that Ciela had suggested and they worked. It was like a game where you tried to see who would give in first.

Suddenly, I saw a little ceramic clown on one of the tables. Of course, I thought again of Krissy. What was she doing now? Would she even care that I was so worried about her?

I was admiring a chess set made of black onyx when I heard a familiar voice behind me.

"Aimee!" Krissy shouted as she ran up behind me. "I was so worried about you!"

I cringed as I thought about facing her. I slowly replaced the chess piece I'd been looking at and turned around.

"Were you?" I asked her sarcastically.

"Of course I was worried, Aimee," she said. "What are you talking about? You weren't in the room. And you didn't leave a note or anything."

"How do you think I felt?" I asked.

"What do you mean?" Krissy asked.

"I woke up and you were gone. I searched the entire hotel. I asked everyone in sight if they'd seen you. I checked the courtyard, the shops, the lobby, outside. I called Dad—and security," I said loudly.

"I don't know why you were so worried, Aimee. I couldn't sleep, so I took a walk. Jim saw me and asked me to go for a short sailboat ride. I was sure that we'd get back before you even woke up," Krissy said.

I turned away from her. My best friend takes off on a boat with a boy. She doesn't tell me and wonders why I might be worried. I couldn't understand this new side of Krissy at all.

"After I'd bothered just about everybody in the whole hotel, I saw you out there on Jim's boat," I said looking at her.

"I'm sorry," Krissy said, putting her hand on my arm. "Will you please forgive me? Besides, now I'm here. And you didn't leave a note either."

Krissy grinned, and I couldn't help but to smile back.

"I was scared to think I would have to search this whole market by myself," Krissy said. "If it hadn't been for Jim..."

I looked over a couple of aisles and there he was. He was busy admiring some colorful pottery on one of the tables.

"Of course," I muttered to myself. "I should have known he'd be here, too."

Krissy didn't hear me. She was busy waving at him to come join us. "I was so glad that Jim knew how to get here. I would have been so lost if it wasn't for him."

I felt some of my anger start to disappear. It was hard for me to be mad at my best friend. I wasn't going to forget what happened today, but maybe I could try to understand it. After all, the Forever Friends eventually forgave me for paying so much attention to Graham.

"I'm sorry for this mess, too," I told her. "Let's forget it, okay?"

Krissy smiled. "Okay."

I surprised myself by smiling at Jim as he joined us.

"Hi," I said. "Thanks for showing Krissy how to get here. This is a great place. We should be fine now. We can find our way home."

"I haven't been here for a while, so I think I'll stick around," Jim said. "Besides, you might need a guide so you won't miss the best parts of the market. Let's go this way," he said, putting a hand on Krissy's arm. "I want you to meet the fruit seller so you can taste the specialty of Veracruz, the mocambo."

Six

I took a deep breath and decided that I would try to be a good sport about having Jim along. If I could make the best of it, then maybe Krissy and I could do something fun together later.

Jim introduced us to the merchants that he liked best. He definitely knew a lot of people. I noticed that he always called us his new American friends. I thought that had a nice ring to it.

He led us to a huge outdoor cafe. He signaled to the waitress and ordered a mocambo for us. In just a few minutes, she came out from the kitchen carrying the largest fruit salad I had ever seen! It was a huge bowl filled with pears, apples, mangos, papayas, melons, and peaches—all piled in a towering pyramid.

"So, what do you think of the mocambo?" Jim asked me between mouthfuls.

"Wow!" I said, wiping some fruit juice from my chin. "I wish we had papayas at home. They're great."

Jim didn't stop his tour there. He took us to the Veracruz Fish Market, where we sampled barbecued oysters and boiled shrimp fresh off the boat. We even teased and dared each other until we had all tasted a bit of conch and octopus.

It felt like we had giggled nonstop for almost an hour. Krissy and I finally waved goodbye to Jim and jumped on the bus. Jim said he had some errands to run for his father. I looked at my watch and saw that we had just enough time to change our clothes and meet Dad for a light dinner.

While we ate, Dad filled us in on his shooting schedule. We were going to the ruins the next day. We had promised Dad that we would talk to kids our age and find out what they liked about seeing the ruins.

I told him all about Ciela and her views on her changing city. Dad got out his notebook and began taking notes on everything I was saying. It was neat. I felt like a real reporter.

Krissy didn't tell Dad about being with Jim all day. And I didn't mention it, either.

We finally crawled into our beds at 11:30. I was beat. I knew the ruins were going to be exciting, and I wanted to be rested for the trip.

I fell asleep reading my guidebook. It felt like a second later when the phone rang. It was the wake-up call we had left earlier. I stumbled across the room to answer it.

"Buenas dias," the operator said cheerfully to wake us up. She was saying "good morning."

"Gracias," I said to thank her for the call. I really didn't feel like thanking her for waking us up, but it wasn't her fault that I was so tired.

"Hey, Krissy," I called softly. "I hate to tell you this, but it's time to get up already."

Krissy didn't move. She didn't say anything.

"Krissy. It's morning!" I tried again. "I can take a shower first if you want. Let me know."

I pulled the curtains open and sunshine filled the room. "Mmm, it's a perfect day, Krissy! Just wait until we see the Temple of the Little Faces. It's supposed to be really cool. Maybe we'll even get enough historical information to write a history paper next year."

"You worry about the paper," Krissy mumbled.

"Hey, we'd better get moving. We promised Dad that we'd help him today. And that's how we got to come on this trip anyway, right?" I asked to remind her.

"I think I'm sick," Krissy said.

Then I noticed how pale she was. She had her hand on her stomach.

"You don't look too well, that's for sure," I admitted.

"I think I'm going to be sick," Krissy said. She ran into the bathroom. She came out a few minutes later and crawled back into bed.

"Maybe I should call Dad," I suggested. "He could probably get a doctor's name from Mr. Stark."

"No, I'll be okay. Just let me rest for a few more minutes," Krissy pleaded. "I really don't like going to doctors."

"Okay," I said. "I'll be right out."

I took a shower and got dressed. When I finished fixing my hair, I went to check on Krissy. She was still lying where I had left her.

"Do you feel any better?" I asked hopefully.

She gave me a weak smile and shook her

head. "My stomach is killing me, and I ache all over," she said. "I'm sorry. Maybe it would help if I ate something."

"I doubt it," I said.

"Why?"

"That pile of food we ate yesterday is probably why your stomach hurts," I said. "We don't usually eat octopus and all that weird stuff at home."

At the mention of octopus, Krissy moaned. "I'm really sick," she said.

I walked over to the phone and quickly dialed Dad's room. He answered on the second ring.

"Dad, Krissy is feeling really sick," I said. "It's her stomach. I think we ate too much yesterday."

"It sounds like a typical case of vacation overload to me," Dad said. "You jumped in and tried everything all at the same time. I'll call room service and have them send up some crackers, soda pop, and manzanilla tea. Maybe one of those will help to settle her stomach."

"So you think Krissy will be okay?" I asked Dad.

"Of course. I think she just needs to rest for a while," Dad said. "You and I can go ahead to the ruins today. I think she'll be fine by tomorrow."

I looked over at Krissy's sweaty face. She was still holding her stomach with one hand. I wanted to do something to help her, but it was probably something that just took some time to go away.

"I hope so, Dad," I said. "Do you think she'll be okay here alone?"

"Well, I'd say it's okay to stay here with her, but I really need your help today," Dad said. "I'll let Mr. Stark know that Krissy isn't feeling well and maybe he'll be able to check on her."

"Okay, Dad," I said.

"Come to my room when you're ready," Dad said.

"See you in a couple minutes," I said, then hung up the phone. "Krissy, Dad is having some crackers sent up to help your stomach. And he's going to tell Mr. Stark that you're sick. So call him if you need anything, okay?"

She nodded slightly.

I put on my tennis shoes and rubbed on some insect repellent. The ruins were supposed to be in the middle of a lot of trees, kind of like a jungle. And I read that there was water everywhere. And that meant bugs would be there, too!

"I hate to leave you alone all day," I said. "Maybe I should let Jim know you're sick. He could check on you."

"No!" Krissy said quickly. "I don't want him to see me sick. I look gross! Just let me sleep. Maybe I'll feel better tonight and we can do something then."

"If you say so," I said, hoping that those plans wouldn't include Jim.

I pulled the sheet up to Krissy's shoulders. I fluffed her pillow up a little so she would be more comfortable. "I'll take lots of pictures of the ruins. You'll feel like you didn't miss out on a thing," I told her. "Remember to call Mr. Stark or the front desk if you need anything, okay?"

Krissy nodded.

* * * * *

It was fun to watch Dad direct the TV equipment and record his narration for the show. He was so serious when he was working.

"The ruins at Zempoala and Tajin are both pre-Columbian," Dad recited into his tape recorder. "They were built by the Totonac Indians during the Classic Period between 300 and 900 A.D."

"Hey, Dad," I interrupted. "I know the ruins are ancient history, but you don't have to make them sound old and boring. Make it fun or people won't want to leave Atlanta and come here."

"Okay, so exactly what do you suggest, Aimee?" Dad asked me.

"Cut the long names and dates. People don't want to be in history class," I said. "Believe me, I know that too well. Why don't you talk to the people who work here and ask them what this place means to them? You could ask them what their favorite stories about the ruins are."

Dad looked interested, so I kept talking. "There could even be some historical story that applies to today. You know, like how crafts are made or traditions are carried on."

I walked over to where people were selling souvenirs. "Look at these dolls, Dad," I said, pointing to an Indian doll with a huge headdress that resembled a sun. "I'm sure this doll represents something. Why don't we ask the dollmaker how she learned to make these dolls and why she does it?"

Dad grinned. He motioned to the cameraman to zoom in on the doll's face for a closeup.

"Okay, Aimee, since you're on a roll today, let's ask her," Dad said.

An interpreter had come along with us in case we needed her. I could make out some Spanish for fun, but when it came to Dad's TV show, I didn't want to misunderstand what anyone was saying.

"*¿Como apprende Usted, hacer estas muñecas?*" I asked the dollmaker.

The artisan's wrinkled face lit up. "It's so nice to see a young girl interested in the work of an old lady," the woman said in Spanish.

"I love making crafts, too," I said. "I've made a lot of dolls by using scraps of material or yarn. I've even made some out of clothespins."

I waited for the interpreter to explain my words to her.

"These are made from scraps of leather, hand-spun wool, and cotton," she explained to us.

"They're beautiful," I told her honestly. "I can tell how hard you worked on them. Have you sold your dolls at the ruins for a long time?"

The woman smiled again. She told us her name was Maria Huasteco. "My family has lived in the town of Cardel for many years. Our ancestors built these temples and were very happy here. We are pleased that tourists come to see and enjoy our history. But it is sad that tourists only see the surface. They do not see the heart."

"Will you show us the heart, Señora Huasteco?" Dad spoke up.

She nodded at the interpreter's words. She stepped in front of us and led the way toward a huge temple. We climbed up and up the old stone steps until we were high above the tree tops. From where we stood, we could see uncovered mounds of other pyramids in the distance. Dad had read that there were many mounds in the forests surrounding Tajin. Those were to be our next stops.

"Do you hear voices?" Señora Huasteco asked us without waiting for an answer. "Thousands of Totanac voices whisper in the wind. They guard the temples. They are loyal."

As this woman continued to talk about her interesting heritage, the Mexican culture began to take on a new meaning for me. Mexico was far more than beaches and colorful clothing. It was a distinct country with a special history all its own.

Señora Huasteco talked about the sun-drenched rock steps and of the struggles of the Indians after the Spanish arrived on the Mexican shores. She told about the battles and how the Aztecs helped to influence the types of structures that were built.

After we finished our talk, I realized that she had said a lot of the same things that Dad had. But the way she described things—from deep in her heart—had made all the difference.

Dad, the interpreter, and I spent the rest of the afternoon talking with people of all ages and backgrounds. Dad would never be able to use all the information, but it was a great excuse to talk with the local people.

In the middle of all our fun, I began to feel guilty. Here we were having a great time and Krissy was sick in bed. I knew she'd rather be at the beach than exploring the ruins, but today she wasn't able to do either.

I decided to make it up to her. If she still felt weak, I would spend the next day at the beach with her. And if Krissy was better, I'd let her choose what she would like to do.

I was glad we weren't fighting anymore. I couldn't wait to get back to the room to tell her my plan.

Seven

WE arrived back at the Hacienda Hotel just before dinner. I really hoped that Krissy had felt well enough to eat something. Maybe we could go sit out by the pool and relax later that evening.

Dad and I thanked the interpreter for her work that day and said good-bye. Then we took the elevator up to our floor.

"I feel like I've climbed thousands of steps today," Dad remarked. "My muscles are really sore."

"If Krissy is feeling better, do you think we could go back to the ruins tomorrow?" I asked hopefully. "Krissy really missed a great day."

"It's possible. But it'd only be for part of the day," Dad pointed out. "I still have lots of things to do while we're here. But I did want to get a shot of the sunrise from over the top of the temple of Ehecatl, God of the Wind. I think it'd be a neat way to lead into the story. I could show a few different sunrise shots as the opening credits roll on the screen."

"And don't forget to include some mariachi music in the background," I suggested. "And you could add some jungle noises, too."

"I think you would make a great production coordinator someday," Dad said with a big grin. "You've been a great help today."

"Thanks, Dad."

"I have to run down to my room and make a couple phone calls. Let me know how Krissy is feeling. We're having dinner with the Starks tonight, remember?" Dad asked.

"Sure, Dad. I'll call you in a few minutes," I promised.

I put my key in the lock and slowly opened the door. I walked past the bathroom and saw that Krissy was sitting on her bed. I quickly dropped my bag on the chair.

"Hey, you're sitting up!" I exclaimed as I searched her face for signs of sickness. She looked pretty healthy to me. "I take it you're feeling better."

"Yes, much better," Krissy said, smiling

brightly. "How was your day?"

"It was wonderful, but I really missed having you there. I worried about you being here in the room by yourself."

"So, what did you do all day?" Krissy asked quickly. "Tell me all about it. Did you meet any interesting people at the ruins?"

I told her all about the neat, elderly woman who made dolls. "She told us all kinds of secrets about the temples that aren't in any guidebook."

"Well, I'm impressed," Krissy said. "I'm not surprised, just impressed. Leave it to you to get the secrets out of people."

"What do you mean?" I asked her.

"You'll talk to anyone about anything," Krissy said. "I wish I could be as talkative as you are."

"You could be if you tried," I told her. "If you pretended that you had your clown suit on all the time, then maybe you wouldn't be afraid to speak up."

"Maybe," Krissy said with a grin. "But it's hard sometimes because you, Joy, and Linda Jean are all such hams."

"What a compliment!" I said and smiled. "Well, I admit that when Dad challenged me today to interview the dollmaker, I was nervous. But I didn't want him to know that, so I did the interview. It's scary for everybody at times, you know."

"Yeah, that's what my sister Kitty says, too," Krissy said. "She said she still gets butterflies sometimes, especially when she's auditioning for something that she really wants." Krissy's younger sister Kitty is an actress—she does commercials and stuff like that.

"Do you think you're up to eating dinner tonight?" I asked. "We're supposed to eat with the Starks, I guess."

"Sure, I'm fine," Krissy said. I noticed a sparkle in her eye again. I knew that she'd probably be staring at Jim across the table all evening.

"Well, I told Dad that I'd let him know if you were going, too," I said, picking up the phone.

I told Dad that we'd meet him at his room in an hour. Then I headed for my second shower of the day. I felt like a mess after hiking through the dusty, humid ruins all day.

"Great," Krissy said cheerfully. "When you come out, I'll tell you about my day."

"Okay," I said as I jumped into the shower.

I tossed Krissy's swimsuit off the shower railing and turned on the water. Then I stepped under the hot water spray. It felt great on my muscles. I tried to clear my head of any thoughts and problems. It was nice to relax under the hot shower.

But then a strange thought hit me. Why was Krissy's swimsuit wet 24 hours after she went swimming last? There was only one answer and my temper was starting to heat up again.

No, Aimee, don't be so short-tempered, I told myself. *Maybe she just went down to the pool a little while ago. Maybe she felt better and needed to get out of the room. She probably went down to the pool alone. You're just jumping to conclusions—maybe she wasn't with Jim.*

I jumped out of the shower and wrapped a towel around me. I wanted to hear about Krissy's day *now*!

I saw that Krissy was already dressed in her new blue sundress. She grabbed her brush and bent forward to remove the tangles from her hair. There were fresh sunburn marks on her back. I began to wonder just how terrible Krissy's day had been.

"So tell me about your day, Krissy," I said.

She turned to look at me. Her eyes sparkled. Then I noticed that she wore new earrings.

"Well," she began. "I ate the crackers your Dad had sent up. Then I slept for about three hours. When I woke up, I still felt weak for a while, but I felt better after a little more rest. I tried to watch TV, but almost everything was in Spanish. And the one English channel was really boring. So, I got dressed and decided to get some fresh air."

"Where'd you go?" I asked.

"To the pool. And guess who was there?" she asked brightly.

"Jim," I said sarcastically. Krissy looked at me strangely.

I felt so stupid for spending my day worrying about her. I had even thought about spending a whole day at the beach just to make her happy. And here she sat with a sunburn and new earrings. I began to wonder whether she had ever been sick at all. Maybe she had made the whole thing up so we'd go to the ruins without her and she could spend the day with Jim.

"Right," Krissy said. "Oh, he's so nice, Aimee. You wouldn't believe it. He even bought me these earrings from one of those people who walk around selling things."

Krissy leaned toward me so I could admire her new dangling shell earrings.

"They're cute," I said.

"Did you know that his father comes to Atlanta on business sometimes?" she asked. "I think Jim was hinting that he would like to visit me. We can write letters to each other, too, just like Joy and Russell do. It'll be so neat. He even invited me to a big barbecue tomorrow night on the beach."

Big deal, I thought. *He probably invited all of the hotel guests to the barbecue.*

"And he stayed with me all day because I told him that I had been sick," Krissy went on. "I'm sure he had plenty of other things to do, but he stuck around."

"Maybe his father pays him to be nice to the guests," I said sharply. "It's important to make a good impression on the tourists, you know."

"He wasn't doing that," Krissy said. "He likes me. I know he does."

I knew I was being mean by implying that Jim didn't really care about her. Maybe he did really care, but I was mad. Krissy had gone off sailing yesterday, and then today she had lied to me about being sick.

"Are you really so sure, Krissy?" I asked angrily.

"Yes, I am," she replied. "We have lots in common. He has a younger brother who drives him crazy. It sounds just like Kitty and me. And Jim's brother Ricky is a soccer champ. That gets on Jim's nerves. He says his parents make him go to all of Ricky's games. Isn't that terrible?"

"Wow, what a bummer!" I said sarcastically. "I think that going to watch my brothers' games is a lot of fun. It's a neat way for a family to do something together."

"Well, maybe your family is different," Krissy said quickly. "Jim has a lot more to deal with than you do. He has to move around and change schools. And he has to deal with two languages and two cultures."

"Yeah, I guess life is rough, isn't it? I'm sorry, Krissy. But I just don't buy it. I don't feel sorry for a guy who has it all," I told her.

Krissy put down her comb and looked at me. She put her hands on her hips. Then she raised her voice a little.

"I'm just telling you all about Jim because

you accused him of baby-sitting me," Krissy said loudly. "He wouldn't have told me all those things if he didn't like me. I think you're just jealous, Aimee Lawrence."

"No, I'm not!" I yelled back. "I'd never be jealous about a guy who has to tell you poor-little-rich-boy stories to get your sympathy. He probably pulls that same act on every cute blond who gets off the plane."

"That's not fair!" Krissy yelled back. "A boy finally likes me and you cut him down. I just don't get it. I don't go around calling Graham names, do I?"

I was standing now, too. "At least Graham is sincere," I defended him. "He didn't tell anyone about his problems with reading. He didn't try to get anybody's sympathy. In fact, I had to find out for myself. Graham's open and honest. Who knows what Jim is all about? He seems like quite an actor to me."

"You are jealous!" Krissy said with a mocking grin. "You don't want me to have any fun, do you? And you especially don't want me to have a boyfriend!"

"Well, for some reason I thought you and I were going to have fun together on this trip," I said truthfully. "But I was wrong. And I bet you faked that whole act this morning. You were never sick at all, were you? You two probably planned the whole thing together so you could get rid of me."

"I was sick, Aimee," Krissy said loudly. "You don't know what you're talking about!"

"We're supposed to be at my Dad's room by now," I said. "We have to be at the Starks' suite in 10 minutes. And I don't want to be late."

"Well, neither do I!" Krissy shouted.

"Of course not. Jim will be there."

I pulled my T-shirt dress over my head and grabbed my brush to fluff up my hair. I grabbed my purse and dropped the room key inside. I noticed that I had forgotten to mail the letter I'd written to Joy, Linda Jean, and Tish during my lunch break. I had decided to send one, even though Krissy hadn't written anything in it and I knew it wouldn't get to Atlanta until after we got home. With the way things had been going, it was pointless to count on her. And writing a travel diary together was impossible.

Well, Krissy and Jim could be Forever Friends for all I cared. I needed friends who I could count on—and they were all at home in Atlanta.

Eight

KRISSY and I walked down the hall to Dad's room without saying anything. I knocked loudly on the door, hoping Dad would answer quickly. He did. And he looked happy. I tried to smile back, but I knew it looked forced.

"Hi, girls. I'm almost ready. Come on in," Dad said. "Krissy, you certainly look like you're feeling okay now. Did the rest help?"

"Yes, I slept most of the morning. When I woke up, I felt a lot better," Krissy said sweetly.

Yeah, she felt so well she decided to spend the whole day with Jim, I wanted to scream. *She was supposed to spend time with me on this trip.*

Dad went into the bathroom to finish getting ready. Krissy and I sat as far apart as we could. I pulled out my letter to the Forever

Friends and read it over again.

Dear Joy,

Veracruz is really neat! The people are so friendly. You would have loved the dancers we watched during our first night here. They wore gorgeous costumes—long, white dresses with sparkles and lace. I've also spent some time on the beach, but nothing could beat the fun times at your pool. I miss you. See you soon.

Love, Aimee.

Dear Tish,

Have you ever thought about learning to do imitations in different languages? Spanish is great. I've had a lot of fun talking to everyone. It's amazing how seventh-grade Spanish is coming in handy here. It's too bad that Krissy doesn't know any Spanish. It would be easier for her to meet the local people if she did. I miss you.

Love, Aimee

Dear Linda Jean,

Help! Krissy is being impossible, and I don't know what to do about it. She met this guy who she really likes, and she completely ignores me. She just goes off and does things with him. Once she scared me to death. I thought she had been kidnapped! I had taken a nap, and when I woke up Krissy was gone. She had taken off with Jim in his boat. Can you believe it? I'm really mad at Krissy right now.

Veracruz is wonderful, though. I met a girl named Ciela and learned how to make corn husk animals.

Love, Aimee.

I reread Linda Jean's portion of my letter, then ripped it up into tiny pieces. It sounded nasty and childish. Everything I had written was true, but I knew that it sounded stupid. Besides, I'd get home before the letter did. And I needed someone to help me now.

Krissy didn't even look at me to see what I was ripping. Suddenly, I was dreading our dinner with the Starks. I wondered how many people would be there. How long would I have to watch Krissy and Jim stare dreamily at each other? Gross!

I thought about having a talk with Dad. Maybe he would have a good idea about handling my problem. If I could just get through dinner, maybe Dad would help me make everything right again. He was my only hope.

"Okay, you two. Let's go," Dad said as he came out of the bathroom.

I picked up my purse and headed out the door. Dad shut it behind us. We followed him to the elevators.

"I hope you weren't too bored today, Krissy," he said.

"No, actually I spent the afternoon talking with Jim Stark," Krissy told him. "He was really sweet to me."

"He sounds like a nice kid," Dad said with a smile. "I'm sure his dad has taught him that it's always best to keep the guests happy."

Dad had said the same thing I had. I knew he wasn't trying to hurt Krissy's feelings. But he probably had no idea that she really liked Jim.

Krissy's grin fell. I gave her a sweet smile to say, *I told you so.* I knew I was being mean, but I couldn't help it. She certainly didn't seem to be worrying about my feelings these days.

As we took the elevator up to the top floor penthouse, Dad talked to fill the silence. He told Krissy that he had decided to go back to the ruins to film the sunrise. She acted like she couldn't wait to go with him.

I thought I was going to be sick. What an actress Krissy was turning out to be!

We walked up to the penthouse door and waited as Dad used the big brass door knocker to let the Starks know we were there. I pasted a smile on my face and tried to look like I was happy to be there. After all, it wasn't their fault that I was miserable. Or was it?

As soon as we had entered the foyer, I noticed that Jim was standing in the hallway. He smiled at Krissy, and she grinned back.

Krissy had been the one who talked about all the changes in our lives. She had been afraid that things were changing too fast, and maybe she was right. I didn't like what was happening now—not if it meant that I would lose my best friend!

The Starks led us out onto their enormous balcony where 10 other guests had gathered. The view from the top floor was really pretty. All the city lights twinkled below, and the breeze felt wonderful.

Mr. and Mrs. Stark and the hotel guests they had invited for dinner seemed to be having a good time. And the food was fantastic! There were Mexican, Spanish, and Indian specialties all laid out before us.

They placed Krissy and me across the table from each other. Amazingly, she was seated right next to Jim. *How perfect*, I thought sarcastically.

Krissy and I ignored each other all during dinner. This vacation was really turning out to be the pits. I kept glancing over at Dad to see if he looked like he was ready to leave. I was hoping to slip out of the Starks' suite soon. I wanted to have a long talk with Dad.

But the adults kept on talking and talking. The sounds of English and Spanish rang in my ears.

No one seemed to notice that I had been quiet all evening. On the other hand, Krissy and Jim had been talking non-stop for more than an hour. They barely even looked at me!

I should have been happy for Krissy. I should have been thrilled that my best friend had met a guy she really liked. I felt so stupid sitting there and not saying anything. It wasn't like me to be quiet, and I felt completely left out. What made me really mad was that Krissy wouldn't even be here in Mexico if I hadn't invited her!

The party started breaking up about 15 minutes later. Finally, Dad walked over to me. "How are you doing, honey?" he asked.

I stood up and led him away from where Krissy and Jim were giggling. "Dad, do you think we could talk after this is over?" I asked. "I really need your help with something."

"Sure, Aimee. But it is getting late and sunrise comes at the break of day, you know," Dad said, reciting the same expression he used to tell me when I was little. I usually smiled when he said that, but tonight it wasn't easy to be happy.

"Funny, Dad," I said impatiently. This is something I really need to talk to you about—and soon."

"Okay, but what about Krissy? Is she involved in your problem?" Dad asked.

"Sort of," I admitted. "Actually, Krissy *is* my problem."

"I see," Dad said. "Well, why don't we go say good-bye to the Starks and get out of here. If Krissy decides to come with us, we'll make an excuse and drop her off at your room. Okay?"

"Sure, Dad," I replied, trying to sound better than I really felt.

Within 10 minutes, we were heading out the front door of the suite. Krissy had told Dad that she wanted to talk with Jim for a while longer. Somehow, I wasn't surprised that she had chosen Jim over me again.

Dad and I took the elevator down to the seventh floor. Soon, I was sitting on Dad's bed and he was pouring me some soda pop.

"So, tell me what's going on," Dad said. "I knew something was wrong when you and Krissy showed up at my room earlier. You didn't even look at each other."

Now that Dad was standing in front of me, I didn't know what to say. Where did I begin to tell him how angry I felt about being pushed aside? How could I tell him that it hurt to be forgotten by my best friend?

I thought I would be able to talk calmly about all that had happened between Krissy and me. But the first words out of my mouth sounded mad.

"Krissy is so ungrateful," I began. "She's messed up the whole trip. We made a list of all the things we wanted to do together. But she's forgotten everything. As soon as she met Jim, it's like she forgot I was here, too. It's not fair."

"Honey, sometimes plans change," Dad said.

"Yeah, and people change, too," I said. "I think that Krissy planned to be sick today so she didn't have to go to the ruins with us. She wanted to be here with Jim. I know it. And yesterday she just left our room to go sailing with Jim. I was taking a nap, and she left. I was scared to death when I woke up and she was gone. We were supposed to be going shopping at the market together."

"Hey, hold on a minute," Dad said as he held up one hand. "I think you should start at the beginning or I'm never going to catch all this."

For the next 15 minutes, I filled Dad in on everything that had happened from the first night when we had met Jim.

"I can't believe how stupid I was to think Krissy had been kidnapped," I said. "I ran around this hotel like an idiot looking for her. And she was off giggling with her new boyfriend! I don't think she was sick at all today either. It's amazing how great she felt as soon as we left."

"That's a pretty big accusation, Aimee," Dad said. "I don't remember Krissy ever lying to you before."

"But she's different now, Dad," I protested. "Krissy even said so herself a couple of days ago. She said that she was worried about going to high school next year and having things change. She said she was ready to meet a special guy."

"I think every girl wants to meet her special guy. Isn't that true?" Dad asked.

I dropped my chin into my hands. "She wasn't supposed to find him on this trip. And I don't think he really likes her anyway. I think he's just paying attention to her because she's a cute tourist. I'm afraid Krissy is going to get hurt."

"That's not your decision to make," Dad said. "And one thing you need to remember is that two people finding that they like each other isn't something that happens on a schedule. Maybe Jim started to pay attention to Krissy at first because she was with us. But he could really like her. That is possible."

"Dad, if I went on a trip with Krissy, I wouldn't ignore her for someone else that I met—no matter how much I liked him."

"Didn't you do that a little when you met Graham?" Dad asked softly. "I remember that some of your friends were upset about how much time you spent with Graham, especially when you first met him. Isn't that right?"

I felt my face growing hot. "But Graham isn't really my boyfriend," I protested. "And besides, he worked with me at the station. He also needed my help in learning how to read."

"Right. But your friends didn't understand that because you didn't talk to them about it. You kept it a secret if I remember correctly."

"I still think it's different, though," I said.

Dad sat back in his chair and sipped his soda. "It seems to me that you have two choices. You can ignore the problem and it will probably get worse. Or you can have a talk with Krissy and try to straighten out your problem together."

My eyes stung. It was hard to hold back the tears. "I don't want to talk to her about Jim. I just want things to be the way they were. I want to see her and do the things we planned to do. I want to spend time together, just the two of us."

"Then you need to tell Krissy that. You need to be honest and tell her how hurt you are feeling," Dad suggested. "And then you need to listen to her side, because I'm sure she's not trying to hurt you on purpose."

"I don't know, Dad. I've never been this mad at her before. But I don't want to lose my best friend, that's for sure."

"I know that sometimes it's hard to see things from someone else's point of view," Dad said. "But I promise you that as you get older, you'll learn that friendships are really important. There will be lots of boys in both of your lives, but it's your friendship that will remain."

I stood up and walked over to my dad. I put my arms around his neck and gave him a big hug.

"Thanks for listening, Dad," I said. "I'll go over now and give it my best shot."

Nine

KRISSY was asleep when I got back to our room. I was too tired to start a deep talk anyway. My head hurt from thinking about everything my dad had said to me about Krissy and Graham.

I knew that what Dad had said made sense. But I still didn't think my friendship with Graham could be compared with Krissy and Jim. I was confused, but I didn't want to think about it anymore. I went to bed and fell asleep pretty quickly.

The phone rang with our wake-up call long before dawn the next morning. I quickly answered the phone and thanked the operator for her call. Krissy dressed in the bathroom. She didn't say a word to me, and I didn't think it was the right time to approach her about Jim. I decided to wait until we got back from the ruins to talk with her.

We rode to the ruins, and the camera crew unloaded their gear. After Dad was sure that the crew had some good shots of the spectacular sunrise, he took us on a boat trip to La Isla de Sacrificios. The Spaniards supposedly witnessed human sacrifices on the island! I wished that there was someone around who could tell us some of the ancient stories about the island. Just being in that creepy place and thinking of all the terrible things that may have happened hundreds of years earlier made my stomach sick. I suddenly felt scared that I might see blood stains or a skull or worse.

I wanted to talk with Krissy to hear if she felt the same way. But she was staring at the water. She didn't look like she cared very much about anything. It was definitely hard to share a tiny boat with my best friend and not talk. But we managed to say nothing to each other.

Being on the ocean suddenly felt appropriate. It was like a big ocean was swelling up between Krissy and me, and I couldn't stop it. I didn't know how to keep the waves from crashing over us and our friendship. If I told her how hurt I was, would that slow the flood, or would things only get worse?

No, they couldn't get worse, I decided.

When we docked on the island, Krissy told Dad that she wanted to stay on the boat and write letters. I think she just didn't want to be near me.

I walked along the paths and looked at all the strange lizards and insects that were crawling around. I sat down on a big rock that jutted out over the water. The tropical breeze felt great.

"You haven't talked to her yet, have you?" Dad asked as he sat down beside me.

"I haven't had a chance, Dad," I said defensively. "I feel awful. It's like a big part of me is gone. Mexico is so gorgeous, but it's no fun without Krissy to share it with me. It's just not the same."

"This is pretty serious," Dad observed. "I still have the same advice, honey. You have to talk with Krissy about how you feel. But you should know that Mr. Stark and Jim are leaving tomorrow morning for Maine. So, you should try to understand what Krissy is going through today."

"So, I'm sure they'll want to see each other a lot today," I said glumly.

"Well, if you don't think you can talk to her now, perhaps you can find a chance tonight after the barbecue," Dad suggested. He put his arm around my shoulder and gave me a little hug.

"Well, I need help from my number one script girl for today's shooting," Dad said, trying to cheer me up. "Let Krissy have her time with Jim today. Then do your best to get your friendship back on track."

"Thanks, Dad," I said, feeling a little better.

Together, we picked out which sights to explore and feature on Dad's TV show. The rest of the day was a whirlwind of activity. After the Isla de Sacrificios, the boat took us to the fort of San Juan de Ulua. It was kind of like a castle, and it had a great view.

From there, we explored two lighthouses and three museums. We finally took a break for lunch.

"Neat place, huh?" I asked as we sat down in the quaint coffeehouse.

"Yeah, I really like the music," Krissy said. The music sounded very tropical. I looked up at her and she smiled a little.

My heart pounded. *Did she want to make up?* I wondered. *Was she going to say that she was sorry?* I had to say something fast before she decided to clam up again.

"Uh, did you get your letters written?" I asked casually.

"Yeah. But I'll probably be home before the letters get there. Oh, well, everyone likes mail, right?"

"Right," I said.

"I sent Kitty a playbill from one of the theaters I passed in town. I thought she'd get a kick out of it, especially since it's in both English and Spanish."

"That was nice of you," I said.

Krissy nodded. "Yeah, Kitty has programs from theaters all over the country. She gets them from her actor pals."

"That's pretty neat. I never knew that."

Then there was silence at our table. Dad had politely left us alone a few minutes earlier to let us talk. He said he was going to talk to the cafe manager about doing a brief interview.

"Isn't it beautiful today?" I asked as cheerfully as I could.

"Yeah, it is. Jim was worried that it might be really windy on the boat. But it doesn't seem windy at all," Krissy said.

"Oh," I said. My stomach felt sick again at the sound of his name.

"He told me that this is the only time of year people can go out to the islands that we visited today. He said that between October and February boats capsize a lot."

"Wow," I answered.

There was more awkward silence.

"I'm ..." we both said at the same time.

"You go first," I said.

"No, you go first," Krissy insisted.

"Well, I just wanted to say ..."

"Chocolate?" the waiter interrupted me.

"Try some. It's great!" Dad said as he came back to the table. "I hope you don't mind if I film you two enjoying yourselves."

Before we could say anything, the bright camera lights went on and the waiter began pouring thick, dark chocolate into the bottom of my glass.

Dad smiled and began talking to the camera. "Here we are at the famous Gran Cafe de la Parroquia near the city of Veracruz. Here with me today is my daughter Aimee and her good friend, Krissy. You may remember these girls from the feature we did on their business, Party Time."

I caught Dad's emphasis on the words *good friend.* I guess Krissy did too, because she looked up at me shyly and grinned.

Dad kept on talking. "We're here today to taste the Parroquia's specialty, cafe con leche. Or, if you prefer, you may order the chocolate con leche."

As if on cue, another waiter appeared at our table with a huge aluminum kettle. He gracefully poured what looked like mud-thick coffee into the bottom of Dad's glass.

"Okay, girls," Dad said, picking up his glass and looking into the camera again. "I've just learned of an interesting tradition. This is the way to ask for milk in the Parroquia."

Dad began banging his spoon on the side of his glass. He motioned for us to do the same thing. Suddenly, another waiter appeared with a second kettle. He poured milk into the coffee and our chocolate until we each told him to stop.

The milk was frothy and warm and full of bubbles. We mixed it up in our glasses. *What a strange way to signal the waiter*, I thought. I didn't think the waitresses at Juliet's Creamery would like it too well. Juliet's was the Forever Friends' favorite place to celebrate after each of our parties.

We smiled and held up our glasses to the cameras. "This assignment has been a joy. Thank you for joining us on our wonderful getaway tour to Veracruz. See you next week on *Weekend Mag*. Good night, everyone."

"So what were you going to say?" Krissy asked softly as soon as the cameras were turned off.

"I'll tell you a little bit later," I said, rolling my eyes at Dad who was motioning for us to come over and meet the manager.

"Okay," she said.

From then on, there was kind of a truce between us. I guess Krissy knew what I was going to say when we were alone. We talked and laughed with Dad about the barbecue that was coming up that evening. And we made a long list of sights that we were hoping to jam into our last two days in Mexico.

I was really looking forward to spending the next couple of days with Krissy. Anything would be fun. We could walk out on the pier, buy souvenirs, or eat pastries from the bakery. I didn't care as long as things were back to normal. I wanted things to be just like they used to be.

Then Krissy messed up everything all over again.

"It's too bad that Jim has to leave tonight," she said. Her mouth started to quiver, and I thought she might cry. "Veracruz just won't be the same without him."

I felt like someone had just kicked the air out of me. *Jim! Jim! Jim!* I screamed to myself. I was so sick of hearing about him. Maybe I shouldn't apologize after all. She was the one who had ignored me—and our friendship.

But then I looked at Krissy's eyes. Tears were streaming down her cheeks. No, we had been best friends for too long to ruin everything over one boy. I put my arm around her shoulder and let her cry.

"Hey, Krissy," I said softly. "Remember, you and Jim still have tonight together."

Ten

I chose a beautiful, knee-length Mexican dress to wear to the party. I really didn't care about the going away feast at all, but I knew it was important to thank Mr. and Mrs. Stark for all they had done for us.

I watched as Krissy curled her hair and put a bright red flower behind her ear. I had to admit that she looked beautiful. But her eyes told the truth. They were puffy and sad because this would be her last night with Jim.

Krissy hadn't asked about my apology again, and it didn't seem like the right time to bring it up. Tonight was her night to say good-bye to Jim, and I didn't want to interfere with that.

I did all the things I had to do at the party that night. I spoke with the Starks and with

Dad. I danced with a boy from California who was on vacation, and I sampled a lot of great food. No matter how hard I tried, I just couldn't get into the festive mood of the evening.

If I heard one more of Jim's corny charm lines, I was going to be sick. But I forced a smile and pretended to like what Jim was saying. I decided to let Krissy have her fun for one more night. Let her dance with him. Maybe he would even kiss her good-bye.

I yawned and decided to go to bed. I said good-night to Krissy and good-bye to Jim. Then I went upstairs to our hotel room.

I had just changed into my nightgown and flipped on the TV when Krissy came bursting through the door. She fell onto her bed and sobbed into her pillow. "Krissy, what happened?" I asked. "What's the matter?"

"Jim didn't even ask for my address," Krissy wailed. "We talked and danced and I thought I was really special to him. But no—he just left. He waved and walked away. No real good-bye. No kiss. Nothing. He never cared about me at all!"

Krissy cried for a long time. I didn't know what to say so I stayed quiet until she was ready to talk. Even though Krissy had ignored me for most of the trip, I still didn't like to see her hurt so badly. I had been right about Jim, but that didn't seem so important anymore. "Krissy, you can always write to him here at the hotel address. I'm sure they could forward your letters to him," I suggested.

She shook her head and started crying all over again. "I couldn't do that. If he wanted me to write, he would have given me his address. He wouldn't have just walked away like that."

"I'm sure there's a good reason for what he did," I said. "Jim really likes you. I know it. He couldn't fake that."

We sat quietly for a while. Krissy stopped crying and closed her eyes. I didn't know if she was sleeping, so I didn't say anything.

"Why are you being so nice to me after the way I've treated you?" Krissy asked suddenly. Her voice was hoarse and barely more than a whisper. She turned over and looked at me with red-rimmed eyes. "I'm really sorry about the way I've acted this week."

I took a deep breath and relaxed my shoulders. "I was really upset that you were spending so much time with Jim," I admitted. "I felt like you were ignoring me and that I didn't matter anymore. It really hurt to feel like I was losing my best friend."

"You never lost me, Aimee," Krissy said.

"It felt like I did," I admitted. "From the first day, I felt like you didn't want to do anything with me. As soon as I took a nap, you were off with Jim on his boat."

"I didn't mean for you to feel like that," Krissy said. "I never planned to scare you to death and make you mad. I really didn't."

"Really?" I asked. "Then what made you sneak off?"

"I really thought I would be back before you woke up," she said. "Aimee, I've never had a boy pay so much attention to me before. I was so excited that I acted like an idiot."

I couldn't help but grin at that remark. "Well...," I said to show that I wasn't going to disagree with her.

Krissy grinned back.

I sighed and rolled over. I propped myself up on one elbow. "I guess we had different ideas of what this trip was all about. I just wanted to spend time together and have fun. At home we're all so busy all the time that we run from meetings to parties. It seems like we don't have gab sessions like we used to. I thought this would be a great chance to do that—to catch up on everything."

"I didn't know that you felt that way," Krissy admitted. "I sort of felt the same way, too, but I was so excited to see all the cute boys and get tan. I wanted to look really pretty when I went home."

"I guess we both should've been more honest from the beginning, huh?" I asked.

"See, things *are* changing," Krissy said. "I was the one who was so worried about growing apart. And then I met Jim and we had a big fight."

"A year ago, life was easier," I said seriously. "There weren't any boys around. We weren't doing parties every weekend and all summer. And Tish wasn't part of our group yet. Things really do change, don't they?"

"Sometimes I wish we could stop time," Krissy mused. "It would be so great for all of us to just take a break from everything and have fun."

"You mean a break from Party Time, too?" I asked. I couldn't believe what Krissy was saying. I felt tired of the business sometimes, but even I wasn't bold enough to say that I needed a break from it.

"Yes, I mean a break from that, too," Krissy admitted.

"Wow, I thought I was the only one who felt that way," I said.

"You want to know something really strange?" Krissy asked me. "I had a dream last night that I was little again. My Mom held me and said everything would be all right. When I woke up in the middle of the night and realized what I had dreamed about, it seemed so stupid. But I guess I feel like that sometimes. Like now—it hurts to grow up. I really like Jim, but obviously he doesn't care at all about me. I can't believe how dumb I was about him."

Tears started flowing down her cheeks again. I walked over and sat down on Krissy's bed. I gave her a big hug and let her cry. And this time, there were tears in my eyes, too.

We talked until after 2:00 a.m. We talked about growing up together, our crushes in grade school, and what it meant to be best friends. We cried, laughed, and talked some more.

The next morning, we left without eating breakfast and walked out to the pier called the Paseo Del Malecon. We hurried so that we would get to see as many sights together as we could.

I pointed across the harbor at the island we had visited the day before. "You should have looked around the island with us yesterday," I told Krissy. "The water was so blue and clear that you could see crabs walking around on the bottom of the ocean."

Krissy looked sad. "I guess I missed a lot of things on this trip," she said.

"Well, you got to be with Jim," I reminded her.

"Yeah, a lot of good that did me," she muttered.

I didn't say anything. We were talking again, but Jim was still not an easy topic for either of us to talk about.

"Oh look, Aimee," Krissy said, pointing to a little boy who was selling sea shells on macrame rope chains. "Let's buy a special memento for our trip. I know it didn't turn out the way we had planned, but we both learned a lot—about a lot of things."

I smiled. The old Krissy was back. We walked over to the boy.

"*Señoritas*, want to buy a pretty necklace?" the little boy asked us. He couldn't have been more than 10 years old.

"*¿Cuanto cuesta?*" Krissy asked the boy to find out the price. She grinned at me. "I guess I did learn a little Spanish while I was here."

The necklaces were less than a dollar each. We spent a few minutes picking out the ones we liked best. I reached into my pocket for some money, but Krissy put her hand out to stop me.

"My treat," she said.

"Big spender," I joked.

"Maybe not a big spender, but I am your best friend," Krissy said, suddenly serious. She paid for the necklaces and handed me the two I had selected. "*Amigos?*" she asked.

Krissy was asking if we were friends again. "*Sí* and yes," I said with a big smile.

"I'm glad. I couldn't stand it if you stopped being my friend, Aimee," Krissy said.

"That will never happen. We're friends forever, remember?" I asked.

Krissy looked at me. "That's what I thought. But then I almost messed everything up."

"It was just as much my fault as yours. I expected you to do everything I wanted on this trip. I guess I can be a little pushy sometimes," I admitted.

"I promise I'll try to never let anything or anyone get in the way of our friendship again," Krissy said. "Not even a little thing like growing up."

"Me, too," I echoed.

But even as I said it, I wondered if we could hold to that promise. Could a special friendship last forever? Would things be the same when Krissy left for high school? What would happen if she met a boy she liked at home? Would she drop me again?

I smiled at her. But inside I wondered what things would be like when we were back in Atlanta. After all that we had said to each other during the past week, I wondered if things would ever really be the same between us again.

About the Author

CINDY SAVAGE remembers what it was like to grow up with Forever Friends of her own. "We shared everything—parties, fun times, getting our ears pierced, talking about boyfriends, and really serious stuff, too. They were my best friends then, and they are still my best friends today."

Cindy's friends call themselves the Grembers of the Moop. They used to make up dances and perform for hospitals and parties—just like the Forever Friends do. One time when one of the girls was announcing their act, she accidentally said, "And another grember of our moop..." instead of member of our group. That name stuck.

Cindy lives with her husband, Greg, and their children, Linda Jean, Laura, Warren, Brian, and Kevin, in northern California. She has a view of the beautiful Sierra Nevada Mountains from her kitchen window. When she's not writing, Cindy is a Girl Scout leader, a dancer, a cookie baker, and homework monitor.